INCH AND ROLY

and the Sunny Day Scare

by Melissa Wiley

illustrated by Ag Jatkowska

READY-TO-READ

Simon Spotlight

New York   London   Toronto   Sydney   New Delhi

For my goddaughter, Vivienne
—M. W.

For Michal and Eddie, for bringing the
sunshine to my life
—A. J.

SIMON SPOTLIGHT
An imprint of Simon & Schuster Children's Publishing Division
1230 Avenue of the Americas, New York, New York 10020
Text copyright © 2014 by Melissa Anne Peterson
Illustrations copyright © 2014 by Ag Jatkowska
SIMON SPOTLIGHT, READY-TO-READ, and colophon are registered trademarks of Simon & Schuster, Inc
For information about special discounts for bulk purchases, please contact Simon & Schuster Special Sales
at 1-866-506-1949 or business@simonandschuster.com.
The Simon & Schuster Speakers Bureau can bring authors to your live event. For more information or to
book an event contact the Simon & Schuster Speakers Bureau at 1-866-248-3049 or visit our website at
www.simonspeakers.com.
Manufactured in the United States of America 0714 LAK
10 9 8 7 6 5 4 3 2
Library of Congress Cataloging-in-Publication Data
Wiley, Melissa.
Inch and Roly and the sunny day scare / by Melissa Wiley ; illustrated by Ag Jatkowska. — First edition.
pages cm. — (Ready-to-read)
Summary: Roly and her friends try to identify an object she finds in the grass, but from their different
perspectives it could be a tunnel, a hill, or even a snake.
[1. Insects—Fiction. 2. Worms—Fiction.] I. Jatkowska, Ag, illustrator. II. Title.
PZ7.W648141mm 2014
[E]—dc23
2013010915
ISBN 978-1-4424-9071-0 (pbk)
ISBN 978-1-4424-9072-7 (hc)
ISBN 978-1-4424-9073-4 (eBook)

Roly Poly saw a
strange thing
in the grass.

"What is this thing?"
Roly asked.
Inchworm took a look.
He saw a dark hole.

"It is a tunnel," said Inch.
"It is a dark tunnel
that drips."

"Let me see," said Beetle.
Beetle looked at the thing.

"It is not a tunnel,"
she said.

"It is a nice green hill."

"Let me see,"
said Dragonfly.
Dragonfly flew up high
and looked down.

"It is not a hill!"

he yelled.

"It is a snake!

It is a big, scary snake!"

"A snake?" asked Beetle.

"Yikes!" said Inch.

"Run!" yelled Beetle.

"Fly!" cried Dragonfly.

"I cannot fly!"
cried Inch.

"Then flee!"
yelled Dragonfly.

"Wait!" cried Roly.

"Do not flee.

Do not fly."

Beetle stopped running.

Dragonfly stopped flying.

Inch stopped fleeing.

They all looked at Roly.

"A thing cannot be a tunnel,
and a hill,
and a snake," said Roly.
"It must be something else."

Roly peeked in the tunnel.

She climbed over the hill.

She rolled along the back
of the snake.

"I know what this thing is," said Roly. "This thing is a hose!"

"A hose?" asked Dragonfly.
"That is not scary,"
said Inch.

"That is a good thing,"
said Beetle.

"Yes," said Roly.
"A hose is a very good thing
when you need a drink.
And after all this yelling,
I am very thirsty!"